SHYKITE STORIES

Fling By The Pool

Contents

Fling By The Pool

The sound of children splashing and playing in the nearest pool grew increasingly quiet compared to the sound of Janet Mcguire's heart beating. She was at the local water park with her boyfriend Paul Thomas and they were getting incredibly close to each other. Their relationship had been extremely chaste compared to their classmates so this was the first time they had even publicly held hands let alone further displays of affection.

'How on Earth had it gotten to this point,' Janet thought?

They had gotten to the park and donned their bathing suits around ten in the morning. It was a busy summer day with lots of children and adults gallivanting about the pools and attractions. Paul had opted for black swim trunks instead of a speedo given his shyness, plus it matched his dark black hair. He was somewhat tall at five foot eleven inches and had solidly built legs from regular soccer practice. All in all, he looked fit and good, not to mention his well-defined six pack of abs that Janet loved to just stare at when he left them exposed. Janet had opted for a light blue bikini that complemented her green eyes and covered her naughty bits but just barely. Her hair was long and curly with a nice chocolate variation of brown striated through. She was lucky her parents hadn't seen her purchase and felt a bit exposed wearing so little in front of other people. She stood at five foot six inches and had a nice curvy body with long legs that went on for days. She was a tantalizing specimen for others to admire from afar but only one person had known the pleasure of admiring up close and personal.

At first, they had run around the park and waited in line for various rides and slides but eventually, they grew tired and wanted a little privacy to themselves. They had commandeered one of the private dressing rooms on the far side of the park where there were fewer people. Paul kissed her almost as soon as the door closed. They had been dating for several months and had gotten used to each other's idiosyncracies. He knew she could hold her breath for much longer than he could so he often initiated and disengaged before she needed to come up for air. Their tongues battled for dominance before eventually lapsing into a more playful tug of war. The victor was Janet, as usual, with her skilled tongue movement. She smirked a bit after they broke apart for air and came forward to suck on his tongue. Paul moaned a bit at the sensations and silently thanked the Lord for his girlfriend.

They continued french kissing for a few more minutes before separating and pulling off their swimwear and setting it on the clothing rack. Janet crouched a bit to reach his still hardening prick. He was already six inches long and quite girthy around. He moaned a bit as he felt her put her hands on his cock, clearly excited for what was to come. He hadn't touched himself at all in recent days in hopes of a little fun with his girlfriend. She leaned forward to lick at his head which caused him to groan with pleasure. She smiled before placing his cock inside of her hot, wet mouth and started sucking gently. She was bobbing gently and almost ready to give him a full-on blowjob when he pulled her off of his cock and simply said, "I think I'm good for now. Any more and I'll definitely cum prematurely. Let's give you a turn now."

Paul then began to gently caress her light pink areola and nipples with his warm fingers. His gentle touch and pleasant grip left Janet quite pleased but she was still aching for more. She took his right hand with her left hand and pulled it towards her waiting pussy. Clearly getting the message, he stroked the outside of her clitoral hood and playfully teased her clit as she struggled to hold back her moans. He masterfully stroked and tantalized her with his touch while simultaneously kissing her neck. After a couple more minutes of play, he was sure she would be sufficiently prepared for more fun and he could feel himself twitching in excitement at the thought of feeling her tight walls gripping his thick, hard cock.

"You want to try something new, babe?" he asked.

"What is it?" she replied.

"I think it would be hot if we let someone else find us in here having sex. You know, exhibitionism and all that?" he suggested.

"I do not know, Paul… What if we get in trouble?" she asked.

"We can get out of here quick if we think it is someone who will report us instead of playing along. It is ok, if you are too worried, we can just do it as secretly as possible," he said.

"If you are sure we can get away in time… then I am down to try it once," she finally decided after half a minute of contemplation.

"God, I love you, Janet," he whispered into her ear.

"I love you too, Paul," she said back.

He reached for the door and left it open just a tad. Enough to leave them visible from the right angle to a single person but not much else. They put their clothes back on halfway in case they needed to run away real quick. Now all they would need is the right person to come along. After getting prepared, Paul slowly stroked his dick and placed it at her opening, pushing aside her bikini bottom. He looked into her eyes and saw that she was ready too and slowly began to push inside her velvet walls. The warm vice of her vagina clamped down against his prick and made him tremble with pleasure. He finally reached the bottom and met her pelvis with his, allowing them to feel each other fully. Paul pulled back a bit and retracted his now fully hard seven-inch length all the while kissing around Janet's neck. She moaned a bit when he began thrusting a bit more quickly and quickly tried to silence herself.

"Keep moaning into my ear, baby," he whispered into her ear. "It is so hot and just makes me want to fuck you harder!"

All Janet could do in response was moan softly and thrust back against his cock. She whispered as loud as she dared, "Does that feel good, Paul?"

He nodded before replying with, "Is it just me, or are you even tighter than usual? My naughty little girl is enjoying being a bit daring, isn't she?"

She nodded back and trembled a bit from the idea of someone catching them in the middle of fucking. "Yes, your little slut is dripping wet and ready for you."

He chuckled a bit and just continued to thrust inside of her, speeding up a bit. He was hoping he could hit just the right pace to keep her on the edge of cumming for as long as possible. He alternated between stretches of long, solid strokes and fast, shallow thrusts designed to frustrate her. The toying with her quim caused her to groan a bit in annoyance, just wanting a solid stretch of full stroked exertions allowing them to both climax. Janet was about to comment on the pace when the sounds of someone approaching their room became louder. For a second, she panicked and prepared to pull up her clothes in a rush but it seemed they were in luck.

The person approaching looked to be a tall, curvy woman with dark ebony hair. She was approaching the room across from their stall. She entered the stall and was about to close the door when she saw them through the gap they had left open. Her mouth dropped open for a bit and she began to blush incredibly quickly. Wanting to make it clear this event was not an accident, Paul quickly resumed thrusting into Janet's incredibly tight quim. He moaned a bit as she convulsed around him in panic and they all continued to make eye contact with each other. After thinking for a second, Janet decided to throw caution to the wind and moaned in tandem with her lover.

Their observer had not expressed any emotion beyond surprise and slight embarrassment at their actions until she opted to begin to remove her own clothes, keeping the door open all the same. She peeled off her white t-shirt and tan shorts to reveal a red string-tied bikini that covered C-cup globes. Her nipples could be seen poking out of the fabric and caused the edges of her areola to be exposed. She moved her hands behind her back and untied the strings holding the red fabric up. This simple movement revealed two crinkled light-brown areolas and nipples for them to admire. Their unknown voyeur tweaked her nipples and moaned quietly on her own as she watched them fuck in the dressing room stall across from her.

Janet felt herself grow wetter from the act of exposing herself to another and felt her inhibitions run wild. She had never been attracted to another woman before but something about the situation left her feeling like she would be open to the touch of this particular woman. She moaned a bit both from Paul's thrusts and the thought of being played with by an older woman. Paul could feel her arousal dripping down his cock and his mind inevitably drifted towards a similar vein. He pictured himself fucking Janet while their voyeur licked and used her fingers to stimulate where they were both connected. He moaned a bit and felt a small spurt of pre-cum come out of his cock.

In the meantime, their voyeur had dropped her bikini bottoms and begun fingering herself. She was moving them back at a frantic pace, clearly aware that this moment may not last all that much longer. She tried to match their thrusts with her fingers and rubbed at her clit with her other hand. She bit her lips to stifle a cry of pleasure that would probably have been too loud for comfort. Each rub and stroke of her fingers left her fingers soaked with juices that she would occasionally pull back to lick off, savoring the flavor and smell of her own arousal. She was clearly comfortable pleasuring herself regularly with the voracity with which she devoured her own cum.

"See that, babe? Would you like to be fed your own juices while you masturbate later?" he asked a little louder to hopefully let their watcher listen in.

"Mmm, hmm. I'm a dirty little slut that likes to drink her own cum," Janet said just as loud.

"I am so proud to be your boyfriend. My little slut here is the hottest thing in town," he said while making eye contact with the woman across from them. "Our new friend here is a close second but nothing will ever beat you," he smiled.

They were both sweating a bit from exertion and incredibly turned on from their dirty talk. They had been fucking for at least fifteen minutes by this point and were ready for a change of pace.

"Let's switch positions. I'll sit on the bench and you ride me while facing the door so you can see just how hot we make our hot, little voyeur," Paul said directly into her ear.

They maneuvered each other around into reverse cowgirl style and pressed his cock against her pussy but not actually going inside. He moved back and forth, dragging his cock in between her labia. Their voyeur licked her lips at the sight of his fully exposed cock, which was covered in precum and vaginal fluid, rubbing against his lover's lower lips. She had also decided to switch positions and had added the act of licking her right nipple, all the while continuing to finger herself. Once all three of them had settled into their new position, it was time to reinsert Paul's dick. He left positioning his cock to Janet's capable hands and just braced for the feel of her tight vice once again capturing his seven-inch long dick.

Janet could feel herself approaching a small orgasm when he hit bottom once again. She spasmed around his cock and moaned a bit in time with her contractions. After she had recovered, she began to bounce up and down on his rigid length, all the while staring at the masturbating voyeur across the hall. She imagined having the guts to call out to their unknown participant to join them and perhaps have her first threesome ever, but her courage failed her for the first time today. 'Another day,' she thought. This was clearly not going to be her last foray into exhibitionism given how good she was feeling.

Their voyeur eyed both of them hungrily and bit her bottom lip to stifle another cry of pleasure as she tried to match their now blistering pace. They had begun to disregard all sense and were approaching their limits as they fucked excitedly. The small claps of bouncing pelvises were the only sounds as all three approached the big apex they had been climbing towards for the past twenty-five minutes. Finally, Paul broke and began to cum first. Hot spurts of white cum cavalcaded down his shaft and up into his girlfriend's womb, prompting her to start her own orgasm. The walls of her pussy clamped down tightly on his cock and squeezed every inch dry. Their voyeur eagerly watched them orgasm and rubbed her clit insistently until she too began to cum, squirting a clear liquid out of her pussy.

All three moaned and groaned a bit as the pleasure overcame them. Juices dribbled out and down their bodies and left them all satiated. This had been a powerful orgasm that would remain strong in their memories for a long time. Janet knew it ranked among her top three orgasms ever and was sure it was the most Paul had ever cum inside her. They had always climaxed together like this due to her parents allowing birth control pills but today had been something special for sure.

"Mmm, babe, how was that for you? Felt like you really enjoyed it," he whispered into her ear.

"Damn right I did. If I thought we could get away with more, I might have asked for round two," she whispered back.

"That was incredible," their unknown voyeur offered at a louder volume. "I haven't been on the other side of a situation like this in a long time."

"Glad we did not offend you by doing this. We were worried you might get us thrown out of the park for indecent behavior or something," Paul replied with a smile.

"No, I was just pleasantly surprised to see a nice young couple in love experimenting with exhibitionism in the middle of a water park," she replied with her own smile.

"First time for us," Janet admitted.

"Ah, the first time is always special. My name is Rosa by the way," she said.

"Glad to meet you, Rosa. Maybe sometime we could try out being the excited voyeur," he joked.

"Or maybe we could do a bit more than watch if there is a next time..." Janet said with a blush on her face. Just admitting that she was attracted to the beautiful woman across the hall somehow left her feeling a little weak-kneed.

"I have a feeling this is going to be the start of a beautiful and long-lasting friendship," Rosa replied with a lusty smile on her face.

Exhibitionist In The Classroom

Was this really happening? Less than an hour ago Jackson Hess had been bored sitting in class waiting for the lecture to be over. It was just another regular day of Advanced Chemistry until he had noticed something a little unusual about one of his classmates. She was sitting in the back row to his left where it was just him and her remaining as the other students had moved forward to get a better look at the professor's messy handwritten notes in the dim lighting. At first, he'd written "it" off as nothing unusual but as "it" continued, he'd slowly come to realize that "it" was indeed something exciting. Those little jerks and twitches he'd observed were indeed coming from a girl's fingers exploring her body in secret.

She was sitting back in her chair with a thin brown jacket covering her upper body and a pair of jeans on her curvy legs. Her legs seemed to be spread a bit and moved slowly about as her hands dipped below the desk, obscuring his view of the exploration he so desired to watch. Her hair was slightly windswept due to the cold air outside but her strawberry red locks looked straight enough otherwise. Jackson had seen Heather Anderson around class beforehand but he had never really spent much time staring at her like now so he was somewhat surprised to see she didn't seem to have any piercings or other jewelry and accessories on her head. She clearly didn't need much to accentuate her obvious beauty but it was common to see other students modify their features regardless of their natural blessings.

Jackson saw her pink lips open to allow her tongue out to lick around her mouth. She was clearly used to pleasuring herself regularly with how quickly she was reaching her crest. He had to adjust his pants a bit as he watched her mouth open and close as she bit down on her bottom lip to mask her quiet moans of pleasure. He could tell it must have been a good orgasm by how long she took to return to normal. After a good minute or two, she opened her brown eyes and took her hands out of her jeans. Furtively taking a peek around the room, she paused as she noticed Jackson's appreciative gaze. He decided to show his appreciation a bit by golf clapping quietly and mouthing encore at her. She blushed heavily before seeming to take a moment to collect herself and put herself back in order. After straightening out her disheveled clothes, Heather decided to tease her audience by putting her still soaked in love juice fingers into her mouth and licking them clean.

That act brought out a quiet moan of appreciation from Jackson. She smirked a bit at the audible noise and decided on the spot that this was a chance to be spontaneous. Heather pulled out a piece of paper and scribbled down "Meet me by the bathroom after class." She passed the note to him and he nodded back in response. He couldn't help but anticipate dirtier and dirtier acts between the two of them as class went by. Mercifully, the class came to a close but he was only brought out of his reverie by the fact that the object of his fantasies was getting out of her chair. She left the class with a quick smile back at him and an enticing sway of her curvy hips.

He hurriedly packed up his notes and followed after her to the nearest men's restroom. She was waiting outside, checking her phone for new messages. She stood at roughly five foot five inches compared to his five-foot nine-inch height. Jackson ran a hand through his short black hair cut in a crew cut style. His hazel eyes glimmered with want as he ran them up and down her figure. She had a noticeable presence with a pale complexion, large D cup breasts, and an ass that wouldn't quit. Her bubble butt was a credit to the gods' divine work creating humanity's finest treasures. Compared to her, he was no slouch, though. He exercised regularly to the point where he had a set of abs that were well-defined and a solid gluteus maximus of his own from playing lots of squash.

"Hey. Heather, right?" he asked excitedly.

"Yeah, you're Jackson, right?" she questioned in response.

"You got me. Jackson Hess at your service," he smiled back.

"Well, you ready to 'service' me?" she asked with a tellingly mischievous grin.

"You know it!" he exclaimed. "Where are we headed?" he asked.

"My roommate is probably still at home due to her class schedule, so we can go to yours?" she asked.

"I think my roommate is also at home at the moment. He's a bit of a lazy bum if I'm honest. So it's probably best to avoid my place too."

"Well, there go my plans…" she said with a dejected tone. Suddenly she regained her mischievous smile and said, "Just had a thought, if you're up for it, we can do it right here in the boy's restroom."

He gulped a bit and thought over the options: pass up whatever would happen for now to hopefully get a more comfortable location at some point down the line or go for it and potentially get caught. Mind made up, he said, "I'm down if you are. It would be my first time doing something so public but after watching you today, I've gotten a bit of a taste for dangerous activities."

"Excellent! Let's get started then, Jackson," she said with a beautiful smile wide on her face.

They both went inside the bathroom and quickly checked for anyone still using the bathroom. It seemed like no one was there and the next class had already begun so they searched for the largest stall possible. Luckily, the largest stall was pretty sizable due to it being designed for handicapped users. They quickly took their things and placed them against the wall. Heather removed her jacket and revealed a white blouse with brown accents. Underneath the blouse you could just make out the hints of a red brassiere. Jackson removed his own black jacket and showed that he was wearing a tight t-shirt. He quickly pulled it off and revealed his chiseled abs. Like tit for tat, she quickly pulled off her own blouse to reveal pale white skin below and a taut stomach. She reached behind her back to remove her bra and exposed her D cup breasts. They were round and full with small quarter-sized light brown areolas. Her nipples were slightly distended from arousal and hard at the tips.

"Ever had a boobjob before?" she asked with a grin.

"No, never. Always wanted one but my previous partners were never interested," he replied.

"Well, today's your lucky day because I love giving boobjobs," she said.

"Can't wait! Let me show you what you're working with," he chuckled before revealing a seven-inch long, approaching rock-hard cock. He was dripping a bit of precum from the tip as he stroked it a bit to get fully erect.

"Wow! I can't imagine having any complaints from exes with a monster like that," she said as she eyed his dick with excitement and arousal.

"Yeah, I've always impressed in the past. Here's hoping it serves me well now," he chuckled. After a bit of stroking, he had reached his fully erect state and was so hard he could swear he could hammer in nails with his cock.

"Well, I've got two globes of fun ready to test out so are you ready?" she asked while playing with her tits.

"Definitely," he said. He then sat down on the toilet's lid and spread his legs wide to allow Heather room to kneel down.

As she knelt, she couldn't help but take a lick of his cock. It tasted musky but clean and slightly salty from the precum. She placed her breasts around his length, almost burying it entirely but the head of the cock could still be seen and reached. Heather gathered some spit from her mouth and let it drip down onto his length to provide lubrication for the boobjob. Once she felt it was sufficiently lubed, she began to rub her breasts up and down. She alternated moving sides at first and then once she saw he was enjoying the sensation, she moved both in tandem and licked the exposed portion of his cock with each stroke. The feel of D cup tits rubbing along a cock was brand new to Jackson and he wasn't sure how he had lived without it before.

Nearly reaching his climax as she had sped up a few minutes ago, he said, "I'm about to blow. You ready?"

"Yep!" she replied back before resuming her activities. "Cum for me!"

His cock twitched a bit as he began to cum. His cum arced out in a curved shot mostly going into her mouth and some onto her breasts and face. Quickly gathering the cum that hadn't gone into her mouth, she pooled the white spunk onto her tongue and opened her mouth to show Jackson what she was up to. Having got his attention, he watched as she swallowed his baby batter and he couldn't help but admire this beautiful red-headed girl. She was clearly something special and he wasn't going to let this opportunity miss him.

"So how was your first boobjob? You down to return the favor?" she asked.

"Of course. Whatever you want in return for the pleasure of my first boobjob, which was excellent by the way," he replied.

"Alright, eat my pussy then," she said.

He got off the toilet and let her replace him on the porcelain throne. As she pulled down her jeans, he kneeled down just as she had and ran his hands across her legs before carefully opening her folds. She was dripping with arousal and her love juice was enticing him to begin eating her out. He gingerly began to lick at her hot box and tasted a slightly musky, flowery mix that made his taste buds do a little jig of excitement. Glad she didn't taste dirty or anything else, he picked up the pace of his cunnilingus and began to use his fingers to rub her clit which had decided to show itself after a couple of minutes of licking and the hood had retracted a bit. That simple act caused her to moan and twitch a bit in pleasure.

"YES, right there, Jackson!" she exclaimed. "Keep licking."

He continued licking at her pussy and rubbing her clit as she slowly began to shake. Her orgasm was quickly approaching and nothing was going to stop them from enjoying it together. She continued to moan in the throes of orgasm for at least a minute or two before finally reopening her brown eyes. She had been unable to mask her moans much during the orgasm and Jackson worried for a second about the possibility of someone stumbling into the restroom to check for students performing naughty activities. Thankfully, it seemed no one had heard her cries so he relaxed a bit.

"You enjoyed that, eh?" he smiled at her slightly out-of-it expression.

"Oh, yeah, you have no idea how good a girl's orgasm can feel but let's just say that you have a talent there," she replied.

"So, I'm hard again if you're down for more," he said hoping he would receive a positive response.

"Mmm, I guess you do deserve a shot at more after a performance like that," she said.

"Alright, so what are you in the mood for?" he asked.

"A nice hard fucking would be appropriate, I think," she replied.

"Sounds good to me," he said. "What position do you prefer?" he asked.

"I love cowgirl and getting taken from behind," she said.

"Your wish is my command," he said.

After they talked a bit more, they decided to start with cowgirl so Jackson replaced Heather on the toilet's lid. His rock-hard cock extended from his pelvis upwards in anticipation of entering her tight, hot, and wet pussy. She positioned herself on top of him and directed his prick towards her entrance. She was well-lubricated from their foreplay so she began to sit down upon his cock. The feel of his girthy length stretching her walls out felt incredibly good. She decided to flex her vagina muscles and squeeze a bit which caused him to groan in appreciation. Once he was all the way in, she kissed him with a happy smile on her face. He returned the kiss with aplomb and they began to battle with their tongues.

After they had kissed for a while, Heather began to rotate her hips while simultaneously bouncing up and down. The sensations were absolutely to die for as he let her go to town on him. Each bounce left him wanting more but as she picked up speed, he began to be satiated. Jackson used his strong hands to play with her breasts and rubbed them fondly. Then he nibbled at one nipple as he tweaked the other. She started to cum from the combined feel of his cock inside of her and her breasts being toyed with. The feel of her vagina tightening and spasming around his length nearly caused Jackson to cum as well, but he managed to hold off for the moment.

"So, how was that, Heather?" he asked with a grin on his face.

"Wonderful. Absolutely wonderful," she said with a smile on her own face.

"Time for you to get fucked from behind, eh?" he asked.

"Yes, sir!" she said excitedly.

As she got off his cock, he reached down with his hands to feel her wetness. It was warm and smelled musky which enticed him further. He rose to his feet and gripped his cock with both hands, rubbing her essence on himself even more. He positioned himself behind her plump ass and spread her legs to put himself inside her. He thrust inside with little trouble and paused when he hit bottom. Deciding to take a chance on the hope that she would like dirty talk, he leaned forward and began whispering into her ear, "How does this dirty girl like my rock-hard cock?"

"She loves it!" she exclaimed back.

"Good, because she's about to get as much as she can take right now," he said as he began to thrust back and forth.

Using his hands to continue rubbing her clit and grabbing her left breast with the other hand, he strived to pleasure her as much as possible before he ran out of juice. Picking up speed, he was rapidly approaching the point of no return. She began to moan in conjunction with his thrusts and wailed fairly loudly at least to Jackson's ears. Deciding to end it all, he just needed to know where she wanted him to cum and hope for the best from there.

"Where do you want me to cum?" he panted.

"Cum inside me. I'm on birth control," she replied.

"I'm cumming," they both cried out.

As cum spilled out of both of them, he couldn't help but grin to himself. Never would Jackson have imagined himself capable of having sex in a public place like this. He had a sneaking suspicion Heather was a little more used to it but he could definitely get used to it. He pulled out of her once all his cum had been emptied and reached for some toilet paper. He was about to hand the paper to her when she instead chose to cup her hands around her pussy and gather the creampie. He watched in slightly shocked silence as she chose to swallow their combined essences. None of his previous encounters had ever been so bold and open about their desires. This one was sure to stay with him for a long time.

"So, same time next week?" he asked cheekily.

"How about two days from now, stud?" she asked in response.

"Deal."

Back Of The Class

Inside the girl's restroom, two horny college students were just getting started. Soft, full lips pressed gently against a hard member, skillfully teasing it to full rigidity. Her wet tongue peeking out from inside to caress the twitching rod, seeking out the little drops of pre-cum that had begun dribbling out of it. Each one tasted a little bitter and salty but the small discomfort brought about by the taste was worth it as she heard her partner groan gratefully. His hands couldn't help but become lightly entangled within her chocolate brown locks as he moved them in time with her ministrations. She was unable to fit his entire dick down her throat, but she was more than skilled enough to make the most of her available options. She wrapped her tongue around the head of his cock and traced a pulsing vein, hinting at an imminent explosion of semen in her mouth.

"I'm gonna cum," he whispered hurriedly, unsure of how much longer he would actually last. She placed one hand around the base of his member and quickly jerked him off while sucking even harder at the tip, using her second hand to play with her pussy. His semen came gushing out in spurts of white, creamy liquid across the flat of her tongue. He came nearly enough to cover the entire bottom of her mouth with quick sighs of pleasure coming out from the now satisfied young man. "I can't believe we just did that," he said with a reverential tone, making it clear she'd made a favorable impression on him. It took her a few seconds to swallow the load before she stood and faced her impromptu sexual partner.

"We're not done yet! You've still got to repay the favor somehow," she replied with clear passion showing on her face. She glanced at her phone for a quick check of the time, seeming satisfied that she had the time to spare. "When's your next class?" she asked. "Don't want to keep my new playmate too long since we are skipping at least one class today. Although, I'm already drenched from the vibes in my pussy and what we just did, so maybe a little punishment is in order…" she trailed off.

"Don't have any classes for the next couple hours, so your wish is my command, my lady," he said with a wink. "I'm looking forward to whatever it is you have in mind already."

"That's right, slave," she teased playfully. For what felt like the tenth time this afternoon, Ryan wondered what luck had led this encounter to proceed so favorably in the first place. He had entered the classroom a little later than usual, running about ten minutes late, and so he had opted to sit further back than normal in order to not disturb the rest of the already entrenched students. Luckily this class felt like it was designed to be easy and featured a lot of simple assignments, which it seemed today was another one to mark off the calendar. Everyone was just watching a documentary about rare, natural stones inside of a dark cave. As a result, there was barely enough light to see with all the primary lights turned off.

His chosen seat had only one other student sitting nearby. He could only really see her silhouette but he suspected it was the same girl who always sat far back and kept mostly to herself. She was roughly 5'5" or 165 cm, had luscious brunette locks that were a deep, rich brown, had a cute button nose, light blue eyes, and boasted close to an hourglass figure. He'd been aware of her for a while and he tried not to stare a few times, but it had been to no avail. He just kept picturing her next to him in his dreams, thinking they would look great together. His 5'8" or 173 cm build with broad shoulders, a strong square jaw, golden blonde hair, soft brown eyes, and taut muscles all over his body.

He was just about to pull out a piece of paper to doodle on when he heard the very faint noise of vibrations. Thinking it was just the mystery girl's phone or something, he waited for it to stop but after it continued unabated for thirty more seconds he took a closer look at her silhouette, seeing she didn't seem to be playing with her phone or any other reasonable explanation at first glance. Her head was down on the desk and seemed like she might be resting. He got a better look at the front of her face when the documentary switched to a brighter background for a few brief seconds and noticed she was slightly red-faced and looked out of breath. Ryan may not have been the brightest bulb in the box but anyone could put two and two together to see that something seemed to be wrong with her. He cautiously approached her from her right side and whispered, "Hey, are you okay?"

She startled from his sudden closeness and nodded her head quickly to indicate she was fine. Unwilling to let it go so easily, Ryan asked again, "Are you sure? I can see you're red-faced and you look out of breath. Would you like some help to the school nurse's office?" She shook her head but seemed to truly consider him for the first time. The noise of the vibrations had gotten a bit louder once he had approached her, so Ryan was now fairly confident that she was responsible for them in some way. It took him around twenty seconds of thought before he figured out what fit all the clues, though. "No way, are you doing what I think you're doing then?" he whispered excitedly.

She turned to face him head-on with alarm in her eyes and spoke aloud for the first time, "What would that be?"

"Masturbating, of course," he said calmly. She blushed and gawked at him for a full 30 seconds before she did anything else. The shock that some stranger would approach her and suggest she was masturbating in public must have been too much for her, going by her continued stunned shock. He was about to apologize and go back to his seat when she finally said something back.

"Come with me, now," she hissed. She grabbed his hand and led him to the back of the classroom and outside the door before continuing their conversation. As soon as the door closed fully, she turned on him and said, "You're the first person to ever catch me in public. I should have known the vibes were too much. Ugh, this is going to suck so much, but I guess that's the price I have to pay for being an exhibitionist." She then muttered beneath her breath to herself and paced back and forth, "What should I do now?" Finally, she came to some sort of decision and looked back at Ryan appraisingly. "Could be worse, much worse. At least I got lucky with who discovered me. Follow me."

She led him to a girl's restroom on the same floor, entering it quickly to check for anyone else before bringing him inside as well. She kissed him roughly on the lips right after they both entered the same stall, taking what she seemed to want for granted, although Ryan certainly didn't mind, not when he was getting his dreams fulfilled at the moment. Now that they were in the light, he could clearly see her outfit of a grey hoodie, denim skirt, and black leather boots. He gently pulled down her skirt to reveal her skimpy thong underneath and pushed aside the fabric covering her pussy to allow his fingers room to roam, each dexterous digit rubbing and infiltrating the warm, tight cavity. He could feel the powerful vibrations of two small bullet vibes inside her pussy making it even slicker by the second. She pulled down his jeans as well, preparing for her own ministrations. She slowly licked around her mouth to entice him into sticking his cock down her throat. It worked just as well as it would on any red-blooded male.

After the blowjob wrapped up, they both stood up and prepared for phase two. Ryan's refractory period was very small given just how hot he found the current scenario. He had been dreaming about her for weeks already and the fruition of all those fantasies was better than he had ever hoped for. He took his already hardened cock into his hands and aimed it towards her glistening muff. Ryan left it up to her how fast to proceed as he wanted her to be happy. It turned out that she wanted it quite rough and told him so directly by plunging herself onto his meat stick. Her labia stretching around his dick in a gentle caress, their hips worked in tandem to increase their pleasure. Each stroke was accompanied by grunts of pleasure and little whines of satisfaction.

"Fuck me harder," she ordered. Ryan gladly obliged and started thrusting as hard as could within the limits of a bathroom stall. "Play with my clit," she said. Ryan reached around her for one of the bullet vibes and used it to lightly touch upon her clitoris, making her squirm with delight. The pleasant sensations of the vibrating toy were just what the doctor ordered. Each thrust along with the sex toy's gyrations left her in a perpetual state of near climax, just as intended. A particularly hard thrust caused her to go over the edge and orgasm spectacularly, sending waves of cum out of her cunt. The tight contractions of her climax nearly caused Ryan to cum as well, but he managed to hold off for the moment.

He kept up his furious pace of fucking all through her climax, even as her legs started to waver a bit. This prompted a position change from standing up frontal to sitting on the toilet and having her ride him, allowing Ryan to lift her up and down his cock. It was magnificently arousing, seeing this beautiful girl's flushed face and sweaty body writhe along his member. Each lift became more and more tiring, though, and he finally had to stop after recognizing his impending orgasm. She had recovered a bit more by that point so they switched to doggy style standing up, allowing Ryan extra access to her curvy booty. He wrapped his hands around her butt with a delicate touch and significant care, focusing on caressing around her pussy and her asshole. Each orifice had intriguing possibilities in its own right but right now he needed to focus on keeping himself from cumming too soon.

He opted to aim instead for getting her to orgasm once more instead of prolonging his erection much further. Using the vibes to playfully touch upon her clitoris and pussy lips, he felt her begin to shake once more. The fluctuations of her pussy left him gasping for breath after he came all over the insides of the gorgeous brunette. Finally, he'd done his job. He quickly glanced at his phone and saw that they'd spent the past thirty minutes fucking inside of the restroom. They still had ten minutes left to get back to class but they would probably be better off just packing their stuff up and heading to their dorms in order to clean up. He wouldn't want to go through a whole day smelling of sex and sweat.

He gently grabbed her shoulders and shook her awake, smiling at seeing the pleased expression still stuck on her face. "We'd better go pick up our stuff. Class is nearly over."

"Oh, alright," she said with a slight hint of confusion at what was going on at first before she remembered what she had been doing for the past hour.

"So what's your name again, slave?" she playfully asked.

"Ryan. And yours, my lady?" he said returning the favor in kind.

"Mandy. So was that as good for you as it was for me or what?" she asked jokingly.

"Better than good. It was perfect," he said while slowly extending his hands towards her face to brush a few locks of hair off her face. "I think we've really got some chemistry."

"Yeah, we definitely do, Ryan. Let's swap phones and put our numbers in," she said with a small blush on her face as she finally addressed her partner by name. "So see you next week?"

"How about I see you this Saturday instead, Mandy?" he counter-offered.

"I can agree to that so long as you keep the back of the class our little secret, now and forever."

"Deal. I'll catch you on Saturday. Oh, and one more thing, wear the same 'outfit' you wore today," he said, pointing at the vibes and the drenched thong lying on the floor before leaving the girl in the bathroom by herself. "Can't wait to see where our relationship goes from here," he said then began whistling cheerfully.

Entranced by an Exhibitionist: Eagerly Enticed

"Okay, class, today we'll be watching the first part of a six-episode documentary about Michigan's rich environmental diversity. Today's episode covers what we know about our state from before colonization and you will be quizzed over the entire documentary later so pay attention! Turn off all devices before we start the movie or you know what will happen." The assistant teacher for Intro to Environmental Science went to start the film after shutting off the overhead lights. Beams of white came from a few students' still active phones and laptops before they hurriedly shut them off. With only the first couple rows anywhere close to full, any distracted students were bound to lose their precious electronics as punishment.

A muted noise came from the back of the room as the door opened just enough to allow a skinny male body to squeeze through. He quickly stumbled into the darkness, opting to find a seat near the back instead of continuing to fumble about. There was one vaguely human shape in the middle of the last row but he couldn't see much beyond an outline which had long hair and soft curves that seemed to indicate they were a female classmate. Opting to sit a few places down from the feminine silhouette, Josh quickly pulled out his phone to ask his friends if he had missed anything. He saw a few notifications from their group chat, which he quickly opened. Reading through them from top to bottom, Paul simply asked, "Where r u? Class started 5 min ago." Dom chimed in with "Teach seems strict. U dun wanna be absent from da start & get on her bad side." And lastly, Nick said, "If ur just running l8 rmbr quiz on long-ass doc l8r."

Before he could even type half a response he heard from the front, "Turn your phone off now or I will come up there, young man." He sheepishly put his phone away and shifted his eyes back towards the projector screen. The slow-paced documentary hadn't managed to go through the opening credit sequence yet and quickly lost its grip on Josh's attention. He looked around to see if he could pick out his friends sitting below but it was incredibly hard to distinguish anyone without consistent light. Giving up on that endeavor, his gaze moved left to take another glance at the other student in his row. With the distance reduced and a bit more light starting to refract around the room from the documentary finally changing scenes to a brighter nature shot, he could now see more of the female figure.

Long, dirty blonde tresses fell in gentle waves around her face, framing a cute button nose and very light brown, perhaps hazel eyes. The shades of brown in her hair seemed to blend into the solid blond strands without looking like bad hair dye so she was most likely running au naturel. There was definitely a slight hint of European descent, perhaps a Scandinavian ancestor's influence on her features based on the hair color. Josh hadn't seen any girl this beautiful before in person and he definitely couldn't help being just a tad enamored at first sight. Although, he cut his fantasy short when he compared himself to her and found his appearance too typical to even attempt to interact with someone that incredible. Heck, she could definitely compete, if not outright decimate, anyone in the whole town or even the state. Her stunning looks really didn't fit into the small community college classroom that hadn't been updated in sixty years except for one out of place element.

The only word he could find to describe her style was odd… it was certainly a little unusual for the times and would have drawn many curious looks in a crowded place. While her outfit did not immediately detract from her overall appeal neither did it fit the face that had captivated him so. An incredibly puffy, light purple jacket, opened halfway to reveal a sleeved solid yellow blouse and a matching purple skirt that seemed to go far past her knees. The last time he'd seen a hem that low was the family reunion with his octogenarian Grammy where he'd seen photos of her younger years and even she'd moved on from them eventually. Moving his eyes back to her face for a final glimpse of perfection, he saw a set of eyes staring back at him.

'Oh, shit!' he exclaimed mentally. Josh immediately realized he'd made the mistake of admiring too long for comfort. He expected some sort of disapproval and began to chastise himself thoroughly. However, nothing seemed to happen: no moving further down the row, no scoff, or even just outright ignoring him with disdain in her eyes. She continued to return his now sheepish gaze with a small, encouraging smile if anything. Baffled that a co-ed this incredible seemed to be fine with his faux pas, he couldn't even pretend to care about the droning of the documentary in the background. Devouring her willing form while she gifted him this opportunity would be the only appropriate course of action.

The dirty blonde looked around furtively to see if anyone else was paying any attention to the happenings in the back. The head teacher had only taken a single glimpse around the room before deeming it acceptable and was occupied with some sort of paperwork, which she eyed with a bittersweet expression on her face. Everyone else was facing the screen except for the two of them and seemed to be engrossed in the bounty of Michigan's lakes. As she turned back to Josh, her eyes mischievously twinkled and she held a finger up to her plump lips in the shh gesture, while using her other hand to slowly begin extricating her arms from her jacket. However, to her appreciative observer's surprise, her hands didn't stop at just removing an outer layer and slowly began to circle the top button of her yellow blouse. Sensuously rubbing the buttons prior to teasing them out of their respective slits, she continued to peer straight into Josh's awestruck eyes.

He could have been struck by lightning at that very moment and he would have been unable to move his eyes away; he was her spellbound captive and she was his teasing tormentor. He quickly took a few breaths to try and recover from the sudden shock of seeing his first naked girl. Having removed enough buttons to see the tops of a typical bra, he was perplexed to only see unending swatches of skin. One more button removed revealed her unblemished breasts with roughly quarter-sized, light pink areolae. They looked to be just a tad more than a handful but both breasts were still high on her chest and looked firm yet soft. Breasts that perky were unfit for any captor and the mere thought of unworthy fabric touching these God-sends made him absurdly jealous and turned on.

Her fingers slowly traced around her raised nipples, winding in a path reminiscent of a bumblebee's chaotic yet purposefully random flight before ending on a blooming flower. Having found her targets, she began softly pinching and teasing her nipples while closing her eyes as the pleasure overwhelmed her senses. Josh would have sworn time was frozen as he strained his ears to hear her restrained moans and gasps; this had to be a delusion, right? Any time now he'd presumably wake up in bed with a sticky mess and relegate this fantasy to the permanent spank bank. He'd never had a fantasy of this sort before but he was sure it would be a recurring blaze after such an intense spark. Either way, this turned out, real or dream, his jeans were currently painfully tight and he adjusted his throbbing length to reduce the pressure.

By some long-forgotten prayer had to have paid off: the erotic display of female masturbation didn't seem to be approaching the end but her fingers seemed lackadaisical as they finished teasing her bosom. Leisurely and deliberately, the digits trailed downwards towards the edges of her skirt. She unlatched the hooks holding her skirt up and undulated her body carefully to slowly wiggle out with as little noise as feasible. As the fabric revealed more and more of her body, Josh kept looking back and forth between her eyes and the ever-encroaching slice of heaven being exposed. Her expression was mischievous with lightly twinkling eyes struggling to stay open as her arousal lingered.

While the lengthy skirt fell, he worked himself into a fever imagining what would cover his goddess; whether it was plain white panties, striped, tied, or any other kind he knew of, his arousal could not be stopped. Once more Josh was surprised by the once demurely dressed classmate when the skirt dropped fully and he spotted no signs of fabric at all. In fact, it looked like she didn't have any hair for natural cover and her skin didn't seem to have any paleness or tanned patches. This revelation made the fervor of lust he was experiencing reach unbearable levels. For a few seconds, he became aware of an intense rhythmic sound that filled his eardrums: his pounding heartbeat was overwhelming his senses and seemed liable to end in a premature heart attack if he didn't calm down soon. He shook his head strongly to clear any extraneous thoughts and breathed deeply before refocusing on her movements.

However, that brief pause barely affected the blood that had been rushing to his member for several minutes. The acute throbs encouraged him to join the denuding process and lower his jeans if only to relieve his aching cock a little. He was about to remove his pants with no heed of the resulting noise when he saw her hands urgently move back to her face once more in the shh gesture. Reminded of the surroundings, he pulled the zipper as painstakingly as possible to reveal his erect dick. A small stream of precum slowly drizzled down the rigid length, providing a small amount of lubrication to the approximately fifteen centimeters long, five centimeters wide dick. As one hand firmly grasped his cock, he gestured with the other to continue her foreplay.

The mostly uncovered blonde smirked a little, obviously amused by how enraptured and horny her lone audience member had grown. Instead of immediately returning her fingers to their previous task hidden below the table, she turned in her seat to face Josh. The switch in orientation left her partially splayed vagina visible for the first time. The medium pink lips were glistening with moisture and extended to reveal the inside labia. Her clitoral hood had pulled back, proudly displaying its hidden treasure. One hand slowly rubbed and played with her clitoris as the other fingers held open her outer lips to allow the remaining fingers increased access. She started with just her index finger and undulated it inside her tight tunnel with deliberate pauses. However, upon seeing that Josh was still just holding his cock tightly, she stopped her play and performed a repetitive jerking gesture while simultaneously inserting her finger.

Understanding the idea and wanting to relieve his own lust, he began to jack off at the same pace as her masturbation. The sensation of touching himself had never felt this good before; he was already struggling to contain his impending orgasm but he attempted to maintain intensity as she added more fingers. He took several breaks to stop himself when his imminent eruption was all but certain but rejoined at the same pace as soon as he felt able. Finally, she seemed to lose her composure and rubbed her slightly red clitoris incredibly fast. Sensing she was about to cum he let his hands move as quickly as possible and pleasured himself to the most intense climax he'd ever had. His entire vision went white with spots of flashing colors, brief visions of his partner, and bright lights emerging before he came back down from his orgasmic high.

His eyes slowly opened to take in the erotic carnage of their session. His cum had fortunately not shot particularly far and mostly covered his cock and underwear in thick, sticky clumps. He turned to his mutual masturbation partner and saw her form slightly slumped over but her arms were clearly still moving though at a much lighter speed. Her eyes were unfocused and hazy as she trembled from continued aftershocks yet her facial features beamed with complete satisfaction.

He gently tapped the table in front of him, which eventually caught her attention. Focusing on the now pronounced blush on her face, he deliberately moved his hands to pinch his legs tightly. The pain didn't make the vision of eroticism fade or change in any way but it did bring him back to the unbelievable reality of the moment. He'd been entranced by an exquisite classmate; she had started pleasuring herself less than two meters away from him while both of them were still in the same room as at least twenty other people; he had just peaked at the same time as her; and lastly, he was reasonably sure they had both had discovered an intensity to climax they'd never felt before. This was absurdly odd compared to Josh's prior sexual history, to say the least. The return to reality left him extremely lightheaded and his head swayed for a bit before slumping onto the table in front of him. Just before he fainted, he heard what sounded like "Thanks."

A surprisingly loud crash from the front of the room woke Josh up. His head rose up jarringly and he quickly turned to look around for the source. After realizing it was just the audio from the documentary, which was depicting a historic earthquake, he relaxed a bit and checked the time surreptitiously. There were still twenty minutes left in the class; he had only passed out for a fairly short amount of time which was a big relief. Remembering the cause of his fainting spell, he immediately rotated roughly ninety degrees to the left and attempted to find his striking playmate again.

To his horror, her seat was empty with no sign of anyone sitting there previously. Perhaps even more surprising considering he had fainted while still sullied with his own ejaculate, his spot was also clean with no sign of anything untoward. His pants were zipped up and even the expected feeling of dried cum wasn't there, although a very slight and unusual wetness still lingered which he'd have to clean off after the class. Slumping into his seat, he lamented his poor fortune. While it wasn't just a dream, he'd still missed the greatest opportunity he'd ever had to get with a girl. He'd been right next to an incredibly adventurous and attractive classmate that not only pleasured herself but more importantly seemed to encourage his interest and he'd blown it by fainting before he could ask her out. That should have been his crowning moment due to the luckiest intervention of fate in his life so far, and probably ever, but it was over and done with.

Josh slowly faced forwards again and looked down at the table. He was about to turn his blank gaze on the documentary when he noticed a small folded piece of paper below. Mustering just enough energy to pick up the scrap, he absentmindedly opened the fold to see what was inside. All it said was, "I really enjoyed that. Sit in the same seat next class and maybe we can consider a repeat performance. ;-) -E" He looked around the classroom quickly to see if she was still in the room but he didn't see anyone that looked like her. The handwriting was elegant, clean with small loops and soft strokes that made him want to devour each letter by itself. Josh reread the brief note several times before it fully sunk in and a huge grin beamed forth.

Nothing would stop him from being in the same spot in two days, that's for sure.

Erotica, short stories, and smut.

Sex During The Social Distancing Era
It's difficult to get laid let alone see people during Social Distancing, but for one young couple their relationship begins despite the hassles of the pandemic. Meet Jessica Oneill, a short chocolate haired woman with plentiful assets, and Jason Kirk, a fit and tall soccer player with rock-hard abs and a solid member to boot, as they explore each other's body and have sex during the social distancing era.

Contains straight sex, doggy style, cowgirl, facial, cum swallowing, blowjob, foreplay, and more.

Stuck Studying with Jane
Imminent exams and unexpected cold weather lead to an unusual sexual proposition between estranged childhood friends. Contains Straight Sex, Missionary, Virgins, Kissing, and more.

Blindfolded & Handcuffed : A BDSM Short Story

Contains spanking, straight sex, BDSM (bondage, domination, sadism, and masochism), cunnilingus, and more.

A master and a pet play in a dark bedroom with some new toys. Everyone's wanted to be at the mercy of someone else's whims once in their life, right?

Excerpt: This was her first foray into blindfold and restraint play. She pulled against her padded handcuffs futilely in anticipation of the next touch. After what felt like ages, there came a light tease of her nipples with a feather. The soft, tickling sensation led to her nipple engorging and becoming stiff. Each feathery touch led to shivers and trembling at the point of contact.

"Master, more, please. I can't take this slow pace any longer!" She began to get impatient and plead with her silent assailant for more.

"Have you been a good girl?" came from the right side of the bed.

"Yes, very good," she replied.

"I guess it's time for a reward then," he chuckled…

A Masked Halloween

A Halloween party goes well for a tall, handsome college student. He meets a mysterious woman disguised in a masquerade mask and gown only to discover something about her later on after their night together.

Interrogating The Prisoner: A Race-Play Short

Lin Hu is tasked with retrieving sensitive information from a stubborn, arrogant white guy. She has only two hours left to do so before it might be too late and all cards are on the table. Will she successfully seduce the target into revealing his info or get dominated by him instead?

Contains race play (white male, Asian female WMAF).

Exhibitionist In The Classroom

Catching a naughty classmate masturbating in the back of the classroom has fun implications for a college sophomore.

What would you do when an unusual, alluring classmate catches your eye and you can't look away? Two students share a secret moment in a dark classroom and explore a new sexual fetish. Seduced by a stranger to share unfamiliar sensations and seek a new sexual apex, he was eagerly enticed by an exhibitionist.

Short story contains Exhibitionism, Voyeurism, Cowgirl, Fucked From Behind (Standing Doggy Style), Boobjob, Cunnilingus, Potential for Erotic Romance, Sexually Charged College Students, 18+ Years Recommended.

Back of the Class
Catching a naughty classmate playing with herself in the back of the classroom has fun implications for a college sophomore.

Staring too long at a beautiful classmate leads to some fun times for a college freshman.

These two erotic short stories revolve around exhibitionism and voyeurism.

What would you do when an unusual, alluring classmate catches your eye and you can't look away? When a college freshman is late to the first day of class, fate conspires to interesting results. Two students share a secret moment in a dark classroom and explore a new sexual fetish in silence. Seduced by a stranger to share unfamiliar sensations and seek a new sexual apex, he was eagerly enticed by an exhibitionist.

These short stories contain Exhibitionism, Voyeurism, Potential for Erotic Romance, Sexually Charged College Students, 18+ Years Recommended, Teenagers' Atrocious Texting, & Steamy + Consensual Pleasure Between Strangers.